# The Ants and the Grasshopper

Jackie Walter and Gabriele Antonini

F

It was a beautiful, hot summer's day. Grasshopper was lazing about as usual, singing happily in the shade of a toadstool.

The ants were busy, even though the sun was shining. They were collecting food to keep in their winter store. Then they wouldn't be hungry when the cold, frosty weather came and there was no food to eat outside.

Grasshopper started to giggle when he saw them working so hard.

He hopped down to tease
one of the busy ants.

"Slow down, Ant. It's too hot
to work! The sun is shining
and it's a beautiful day.
Summer will soon be over.
You should be more like me –
just relax and enjoy yourself!"

"You should be finding grain, too!" Ant called back. "There's plenty to eat now, but what will you do in the winter? The ground will be hard and there will be nothing to eat. You'll starve if you have no food in store."

Grasshopper sprang back
up to his leaf and sulked.
"Ants just don't know how
to have fun," he thought.
"There's plenty of time to
worry about food for winter.
It's far too hot to think about
it today!"

That winter was cold. The snow fell thickly on the frozen ground. In their snug den, the ants kept cosy and warm. Their store was full of grain from all their hard work during the summer.

One icy morning, two ants
left their den to go for a walk.
They hadn't gone far when
they heard a soft crying
sound. The ants went to find
out who was sounding so sad.

Grasshopper was shivering under a snowy leaf. He was whimpering and feeling very sorry for himself indeed. He hadn't eaten as much as one tiny seed since the snow had started to fall.

The ants were shocked to see Grasshopper looking so terrible.

"May I have some grain?" Grasshopper begged. "I haven't eaten for weeks. Please!"

"Where is your grain?" the ants asked Grasshopper. "You must have collected some food during the summer. You knew the winter would soon be coming!"

“I was too busy singing,”

said Grasshopper.

"The days were so warm and
I was having so much fun
that I forgot to collect any
food. Then it was too late and
there was no food left to eat."

The ants thought hard. They had worked all summer to make sure they would have food for the winter. Grasshopper had just enjoyed himself and done no work at all.

But they couldn't just leave
Grasshopper in the snow
with no food.

"We will help you, Grasshopper," said the ants. "But next year, you must work like we do in the summer and find your own grain to eat during the winter."

"I will," promised Grasshopper.

# About the story

*The Ant and the Grasshopper* is a fable by Aesop. Aesop was a slave and a storyteller who is believed to have lived in ancient Greece between 620 and 560 BCE, making this story over 2,500 years old. There are many different versions, including a ballet and an opera. A fable is a story that contains a lesson. This story shows the value of hard work and making plans for the future. In the original version, the ant does not help the grasshopper.

## Be in the story!

Imagine you are Grasshopper in the following summer. Are you still lazing about?

Now imagine you are the ants. What will you say to Grasshopper next winter if he still needs your help?

Franklin Watts
First published in Great Britain in 2015 by The Watts Publishing Group



Series Editor: Jackie Hamley
Series Advisor: Catherine Glavina
Series Designer: Cathryn Gilbert

A CIP catalogue record for this book is available from the British Library.

The artwork for this story first appeared in *Tadpoles Tales: The Ant and the Grasshopper*

ISBN 978 1 4451 4452 8 (hbk)
ISBN 978 1 4451 4454 2 (pbk)
ISBN 978 1 4451 4453 5 (library ebook)
ISBN 978 1 4451 4455 9 (ebook)

Printed in China

Franklin Watts
An imprint of
Hachette Children's Group
Part of The Watts Publishing Group
Carmelite House
50 Victoria Embankment
London EC4Y 0DZ

An Hachette UK Company
www.hachette.co.uk

www.franklinwatts.co.uk